STORIES FROM

AFRICA

Folklore of the World

Each of the Folklore of the World Books contains carefully selected myths and folktales most representative of a single country. These books will help children to understand people in other lands and will help them to develop an appreciation for their customs and culture. Peace for the world can come only through the spreading of this understanding and appreciation.

The Folklore Books are the third step in the Dolch program, *Steps to a Lifetime Reading Habit*. The series on these graded steps, starting with the most elementary, are: the First Reading Books, the Basic Vocabulary Books, the Folklore of the World Books, and the Pleasure Reading Books.

Folklore Books are prepared under the direction of Edward W. Dolch, formerly Professor of Education, University of Illinois. In all the series, emphasis is placed on good storytelling and literary quality, as well as on simplicity of vocabulary.

Books in this series are (to date):

STORIES FROM

AFRICA

Folklore of the World

by MARGUERITE P. DOLCH

illustrated by VINCENT D. SMITH

GARRARD PUBLISHING COMPANY
CHAMPAIGN, ILLINOIS

Library of Congress Cataloging in Publication Data

Dolch, Marguerite Pierce, 1891—
    Stories from Africa.

    (Folklore of the world)
    CONTENTS: The hunter in the fog.—How man
and woman were made.—Why we have rain. [etc.]

    1. Tales, African. [1. Folklore—Africa]
I. Smith, Vincent D. II. Title.
PZ8.1.D716St   [E]   75—5888
ISBN 0—8116—2562—1

Foreword

There are many different people living in Africa. They speak many different languages. But they all love to tell stories.

Many of the stories are much like the fairy stories that you have heard. These are some stories from different parts of Africa.

Long ago the people of Africa thought that man could talk with animals. And animals could talk with each other. Man and animals could talk with the Sun and the Moon and the Gods of the Sky Country.

The people in the little villages love to sing and dance. When they wanted to teach their children a lesson, they told a story. They wanted the boys to be good hunters. They wanted the girls to be good wives and to make good gardens.

There are many, many stories that the people of Africa told around the fire. I hope you enjoy reading these stories. Then you can go to the library and get other books about the people of Africa.

MARGUERITE P. DOLCH

Contents

The Hunter in the Fog

A Hunter went hunting in a fog because he was very hungry. But he found no animals. At last he saw a little bird on a bush.

"I will have to shoot that little bird or I will have nothing to eat," said the Hunter.

When the Hunter shot at the bird, he missed it in the fog.

The little bird turned into a fierce Great Bird and began to sing,

1

"He who walks about in the fog
here he comes,
He who walks about in the fog
here he comes.
Out in the fog is a Great Bird
here he comes."

When the Hunter saw the Great
Bird and heard him sing, he ran
away. He ran to Lion.

"Save me Lion, Save me Lion,"
cried the Hunter.

"Why did you come to me," said
Lion.

"I am running away from the
Great Bird," cried the Hunter.
"Listen and you will hear him
sing his song."

The Lion heard the Great Bird singing,

"He who walks about in the fog
   here he comes,
He who walks about in the fog
   here he comes.
Out in the fog is a Great Bird
   here he comes."

The Lion was so afraid that he cried, "Hunter, go away from here."
The Hunter ran to Leopard.
"Save me Leopard. Save me Leopard," cried the Hunter.
"Hunter, why did you come to me?" asked the Leopard.

"I am running away from the
Great Bird," said the Hunter.
"Listen and you will hear him
sing his song."

The Leopard heard the
Great Bird singing,

"He who walks about in the fog
here he comes,
He who walks about in the fog
here he comes.
Out in the fog is a Great Bird
here he comes."

Leopard was so afraid that he
cried, "Hunter go away from here."
The Hunter ran to Tortoise.

"Save me Tortoise. Save me Tortoise," cried the Hunter.

"Hunter, why did you come to me?" asked the Tortoise.

"I am running away from the Great Bird," said the Hunter. "Listen and you will hear him sing his song."

Tortoise heard the Great Bird singing,

"He who walks about in the fog
    here he comes,
He who walks about in the fog
    here he comes.
Out in the fog is a Great Bird
    here he comes."

"Go into my house. I will save you," said the Tortoise. "I am not afraid of the Great Bird."

The Tortoise walked up and down in front of his house. He heard the Great Bird singing. But he was not afraid.

The Great Bird came up to the house of Tortoise. He thought he would push Tortoise aside and go into the house and kill the Hunter. Great Bird caught Tortoise by the tail.

Tortoise pulled in his tail and shut his shell on Great Bird's beak. It hurt Great Bird and he cried loudly.

The animals in the forest heard Great Bird. They came to the house of Tortoise. They sang a song.

"Tortoise is the old, old
Wise One,
Tortoise is the old, old
Wise One.
That is it, That is it,
There, There, That is it."

Tortoise opened his shell. Great Bird was so afraid that he flew away.

That is how the Hunter got away from the Great Bird. He never went hunting in the fog again.

How Man and Woman Were Made

A very long time ago there were only the Moon in the Sky and the Toad in the waters of the Earth.

One day Moon said to Toad, "I see the land is beginning to come upon the Earth. The land is very beautiful with trees and flowers and fruits upon it."

"Yes," said Toad. "I am learning to walk about on the land. It is very beautiful."

"I will make a Man and a Woman to live upon the Earth," said Moon.

"No," said Toad. "I live upon the Earth. And I can make a better Man and a better Woman than you can. You, Moon live in the Sky and will not know how to make a Man and a Woman to live upon the Earth."

"If you make a Man and a Woman they will live on the Earth a little while," said Moon. "Then they will die just as you are going to die some day. But I live forever. And if I make Man and Woman, I will put a little of myself in them."

Moon and Toad talked and talked for a long time.

Moon and Toad could not agree. They became very angry. Moon went up in the Sky, and Toad went to his house on Earth.

Toad stayed in his house and thought how wise he was. He knew he could make people who could live upon the Earth. Toad grew big and bigger as he thought how wise he was. At last he made Man and Woman.

They looked somewhat like Toad.

Toad pushed the two people out of his house and said, "Go and live upon the land."

Man and Woman walked on the land. They did not know what

to do. They did not know that they could eat the fruit. They did not know that they could pick the flowers.

Moon in the Sky saw the Man and the Woman that Toad had made. They were not beautiful for they looked like Toad.

Moon was very angry. He came down to Earth and killed Toad.

Moon went up in the Sky and watched Man and Woman. At last he called to them, and they were afraid.

"Poor things," said Moon. "You cannot live upon the Earth, I must help you."

Moon came down to Earth and put the Man and the Woman into warm water. Moon kept them in the warm water and rubbed them with his hands until they looked like a real Man and a real Woman.

Moon took the people out of the water and blew his breath upon them until they were dry. He put the Man and the Woman upon the land. They were happy this time for they knew what to do.

"You are very beautiful," said Moon. "I will call the Woman Hanna and the Man Bateta. You will have many children to look after you when you are old."

"Bateta and Hanna hear my words," said Moon. "I will give you the Earth and all that is upon the Earth for you and your children.

"I will give you all those things which you need to make you happy.

"Your stay upon Earth will not be long because Toad who lived upon the Earth made you.

"But I made you wise. You will know all things upon the Earth. And your children will know all things that are under the Earth. They will know all things that are in the Sky."

Then Moon showed Bateta and Hanna how to make a fire. Moon showed them how to make a pot so that they could cook their food over the fire.

"Call me and I will help you at any time," said Moon.

The Moon went up into the Sky. And that was the last time that Moon came to the Earth.

Bateta and Hanna lived on the Earth and were very happy.

Why We Have Rain

Osaw who lived in the Sky had a very beautiful Daughter. And Nsi who lived on Earth had a fine Son. One day Nsi sent a messenger to Osaw who said,

"Nsi of Earth sends greetings to Osaw who lives in the Sky. Send me your Daughter Ara that she may be my youngest Wife. I will send you my Son that he may find a wife among your people."

Osaw sent Ara down to Earth with many gifts and seven servants.

For a time Ara was very happy. But one day Nsi said to his youngest Wife, "Go and work on the farm."

"My Father gave me seven servants to work for me," said Ara. "I will send my servants to work on your farm."

Nsi was very angry.

"A Wife should obey her Husband. Go and work on the farm."

Ara went to the farm and when she returned at night, she was very tired.

Nsi said to his youngest Wife, "Go to the river and bring water."

Ara was very tired. She said, "I have worked on the farm all day. I have never done that kind of work before. May I send my servants to the river to get the water?"

Nsi said, "You must obey me."

He made his youngest Wife go to the river and get water.

Ara went to the river for water. She was so tired that she could hardly carry the water jug. And all the way home the tears fell from her eyes.

From that day Nsi made his youngest Wife do all the hard work.

One day when Ara was working on the farm, she got a thorn in her foot. Her foot hurt her very much. When she got home, Nsi made her go for water.

When she got to the river, she put her foot in the cool water and it did not hurt so much.

"Oh Father Osaw," cried Ara, "I cannot live on Earth any longer. I am coming back to the Sky."

All night she sat on the bank of the river and cried. Next morning she set out to find the Sky. She came to a tall tree and saw a rope hanging down.

"I am sure that rope is hanging down from the Sky," said Ara to herself.

She started to climb the rope. She climbed all day and she was only halfway up the rope. She was so tired that she could not stop crying. But Ara kept climbing. She had to get to the Sky.

After a very long time, Ara found herself in her Father's country. She sat down to rest, for she was so tired that she could hardly walk.

One of Osaw's servants was hunting for firewood in the forest. He heard Ara crying.

The servant ran back to the house of Osaw and cried, "I have heard Ara crying in the forest."

Osaw went to the forest and found Ara. He took her to the house of her Mother. Osaw had the servants bring Ara all kinds of good things to eat. Ara's Mother gave her beautiful clothes. But Ara could not stop crying.

Osaw called the Wise Man of his Country. He told him that he must punish Nsi for the way he has treated his Daughter Ara.

"Bring me the Son of Nsi," said the Wise Man. "I will cut off his ears."

When they brought the Son of Nsi to Osaw, he said, "I must punish Nsi for the way he has treated my Daughter Ara."

The Son said, "Do not hurt me for the way my Father treated Ara." And his tears fell down his face.

Then the Wise Man made a powerful Magic. A big wind blew. It blew the tears of Osaw's Daughter and Nsi's Son right down to Earth.

For the first time the Earth had rain.

Be-Thankful Came Home

In a small village by a river
there were many fishermen. They
caught fish every day. The people
got tired of eating fish.

One day some Hunters came to
the village to live. And the
people said,

"We are glad that you came to
our village to live. We are tired
of eating fish. Go to the forest
across the river and kill an
animal for meat. Then we can
have roast meat to eat."

The Hunters went across the river. They went to the village in the forest. They said to the people of the village,

"We have come to kill an animal. The people across the river are tired of eating fish. They have asked us to kill an animal so that they can have meat to eat."

There was a Man in the village who had a wonderful hunting Dog.

The Man said, "If you go hunting in the forest, you will need my Dog to help you hunt."

"We will buy your Dog," said the Hunters, "for we want a dog to help us hunt."

The Hunters bought the Dog.

"Be careful of this Dog," said the Man. "This Dog is more like a man than a dog. He can hunt as well as any man. He always eats his food from a basket like we do. Be thankful that I sold him to you for he is a wonderful Dog."

The Hunters named the Dog Be-Thankful.

The Hunters called to the Dog, "Be-Thankful come with us into the forest and help us hunt."

As the Hunters went deep into the forest, Be-Thankful first killed a wild pig. Then Be-Thankful killed an elephant.

The Hunters had so much meat that they could hardly carry all the meat back to the village.

"The Man was right," said the Hunters. "Be-Thankful is a wonderful hunting dog. He can hunt as well as any man."

The Hunters told the people how Be-Thankful had killed the wild pig. And then the Hunters told the people how Be-Thankful had killed an elephant.

The women said, "Be-Thankful can hunt as well as any man."

The people who lived in the village by the river had more meat than they could eat.

The people beat the drums and
danced around and around.

"Be-Thankful is a wonderful
        Hunter
Be-Thankful is a wonderful
        Hunter
He killed a wild pig
He killed an elephant
So big, So big
Now we will have meat
        to eat."

When Be-Thankful heard the
people singing, he was very proud.
He wagged his tail and barked.
The men made a big fire and

the women cooked the meat. The
people had a great feast. They beat
the drums and sang and danced.

Be-Thankful sat by the fire
and watched the people. He was
very hungry and the meat smelled
so good.

But the women did not give
Be-Thankful any meat to eat. They
put mush on the ground and
Be-Thankful would not eat it.

"I killed a wild pig for the
Hunters of the village. I killed
an elephant so that the people
could have much meat," said
Be-Thankful to himself.

Be-Thankful felt very sad.

"The people of this village do not like me," he said to himself. "The women cooked the meat and the people of the village had a great feast. I was very hungry, but the women did not give me any meat to eat. I am going to run away to the river."

The women saw Be-Thankful running down the road to the river. They ran after him. They cried, "Be-Thankful come back. Be-Thankful come back.

"We are sorry that we did not give you any meat to eat like we gave to the men."

Be-Thankful ran to the river.

Be-Thankful was very sad for the women of the village had not given him any meat to eat. He sat by the river a long time.

Then he began to sing,

"As I am Be-Thankful
I go back to the Hunters
As I am Be-Thankful
I go back to the Hunters
I must go to the village
I can not run away."

The women went back to the village and told the Hunters, "Be-Thankful has run away."

The Hunters were very angry.

"Did you give Be-Thankful meat in a basket?" asked the Hunters.

"No," said the women. "We put mush upon the ground and Be-Thankful would not eat it."

"You must put meat in a basket for Be-Thankful," said the Hunters. Then they saw Be-Thankful coming down the road. He was singing,

"As I am Be-Thankful
I go back to the Hunters
As I am Be-Thankful
I go back to the Hunters
I must go to the village
I can not run away."

After that Be-Thankful always ate meat from a basket.

The Wise Dog

A woman named Kitinda had a Wise Dog. The Dog followed her everywhere she went. When he barked, Kitinda could understand what he was trying to say to her.

One day Kitinda took her palm oil and her chickens to Market. She wanted to get some things for her house.

The Wise Dog went with her. Kitinda and the Dog talked together as they went along the road.

The Dog told Kitinda how much he loved her and how much he wanted to help her.

"I would like to do more for you," said the Dog. "But I am afraid."

"Why are you afraid?" asked Kitinda.

"People believe in Witches," said the Dog. "If I do many wise things, people will look at me and say, 'That is not a dog, that is a Witch!' And then they will burn me. I do not want to be burned."

"Could you do more things for me than you have already done?" asked Kitinda.

"Oh yes," said the Wise Dog. "But if you told the people they would look at me and say, 'That is not a Dog. That is a Witch.'"

"I would never tell the people anything that you do for me," said Kitinda.

"You are a woman and a woman likes to talk," said the Wise Dog.

Kitinda came to the Marketplace and seated herself among the women of the village. The women talked and talked. She heard all the news of the village. She traded her palm oil and her chickens for many things for her home.

Kitinda had two large jugs and a basket and a bunch of bananas. She had a big sleeping mat and two carved stools. She had a hoe for her garden and a bag of flour.

When the Market was over, Kitinda looked at the many things she had to take back to her home.

"I don't know how I can get these things home," she said to the Wise Dog who sat beside her.

"I can put the sleeping mat and the flour and bananas into the basket. But what am I to do with the stools and the hoe and the two big jugs?"

Wise Dog ran off to the village. He found a Man carrying a long pole. He went up to the Man and licked his hand.

At first the Man was afraid. But Wise Dog wagged his tail and showed the Man that he would not hurt him.

The Man reached down and patted Wise Dog on the head. Then Wise Dog took hold of the Man's hand and pulled him.

"Do you want me to go with you?" asked the Man.

Wise Dog wagged his tail and the Man understood. The Man and Wise Dog went to the Marketplace.

The Man found Kitinda with her many things that she could not carry home.

"I will help you," said the Man, "if you will give two bananas."

The Man tied the stools on one end of his pole. He tied the hoe and the jugs on the other end of his pole. He put the pole on his shoulders. Then off they went to Kitinda's village.

Wise Dog was very proud and walked along with his tail held high.

When they came to the village the people wanted to hear the news from the Marketplace.

The people sat around Kitinda and she talked and talked. At last she said, "I never could have brought my things home if Wise Dog had not gone to the village and got the Man with the pole. He told the Man to come and help me."

A man cried out, "That is not a dog. That is a Witch who has turned herself into a dog."

The man took his knife and was going to kill Wise Dog.

But Wise Dog ran away to the forest. No one ever saw Wise Dog again.

The Hunter Who Was King

Once there was a Hunter who was very poor. He went out hunting every day. But he could hardly find any food.

At last he went to the Man of Magic.

"Tell me, Oh Man of Magic, what is my fortune."

"When you are hunting, take the first thing that you find, even if it is something you do not want," said the Man of Magic. "Be happy with what you have."

The next day the Hunter took his knife and went hunting. He looked and he looked for some animal. At last he found a crocodile. But the Hunter did not want a crocodile.

The Hunter remembered what the Man of Magic had told him, "Take the first thing that you find."

The Hunter ran after the crocodile. But the crocodile ran away into the bushes and went down a hole. When the Hunter came to the hole, he began to dig with his knife. He was not going to let the crocodile get away.

As the hole got bigger, the Hunter began to sink into the hole.

The Hunter went down, down into the Earth. He found himself in a town. There were no men in the town. He saw only women.

The women were surprised to see the Hunter for they had never seen a man. They sang and danced for him.

Then the women took the Hunter to the palace where the Queen lived.

The Queen had her servants make a great feast for the Hunter. And for the first time in his life the Hunter had all he could eat.

Before long the Queen fell in love with the Hunter and they were married. And now the Hunter was a King.

The Queen showed the Hunter every room in her palace.

"You are King now and every thing in the town and in the palace belongs to you," said the Queen.

Then the Queen took the Hunter to a door and said, "You must not open this door."

The Hunter laughed and said, "Everything in the town is mine. Everything in the palace is mine. Why can't I open this door?"

For a long time the Queen and the Hunter were very happy. The Hunter had a beautiful wife, a fine palace, good food, and many servants. He had been very poor and now he was rich.

One day the hunter sat down and said to himself, "I am King. The palace belongs to me and everything in it. The town belongs to me. What is there in the palace or the town that does not belong to me?"

Then the Hunter remembered what the Queen had said, "Everything belongs to you, but you must not open this door."

One day when the Queen was away, the King went to the door and opened it. He was sorry as soon as the door was opened. But it was too late.

The Hunter was standing just where the crocodile had gone down the hole in the ground. He was once more a poor Hunter.

The Hunter went again to the Man of Magic and told him the story of the town and the Queen and the palace.

"I am sorry for what I did," said the Hunter. "Please help me to get back to my Queen and to the palace where I was King."

"You did not remember what I told you," said the Man of Magic. "I told you to be happy with what you had. You had your chance and you lost it because you were not happy with what you had. I cannot help you."

And the Hunter who once was a King and had everything became a poor hunter all the rest of his life.

Kintu

Long ago a beautiful Daughter of the Sky Country came to Earth with her Brother. She saw Kintu and fell in love with him. She wanted to marry Kintu. But Kintu was very poor. The only thing that Kintu had was a cow that gave him all of his food.

The Brother said to his sister, "Nambi, our Father, the King of the Sky Country, would not want you to marry Kintu because he is so poor and only has one cow."

Nambi and her Brother went back to their Father, Gulu, who was King of the Sky Country.

Nambi said to her Father, "I love Kintu, and I want to be his wife."

"We will have to test Kintu," said Gulu. "He must prove that he is a good enough Man to marry the Daughter of the King of the Sky Country."

Gulu told his Son to go down to Earth and steal Kintu's cow and bring it to the Sky Country.

"We shall see if Kintu can get food for himself without his cow," said Gulu.

Kintu could not find his cow. He worked hard and found some leaves and berries that he could eat.

One day Nambi saw Kintu's cow among her Brother's cows in the Sky Country. She went to Earth and told Kintu to come to the Sky Country and get his cow.

Kintu went to the Sky Country. He was very much surprised to see people and houses and cows and goats and chickens in the Sky Country. It was just like Earth only more beautiful.

Kintu went to Nambi's house to thank her for finding his cow.

When Nambi's Brother saw Kintu sitting in his sister's house, he was very angry. He seized Kintu and shut him up in a house by himself. Then he went to his Father and said, "Kintu is here in the Sky Country. He wants to marry my sister, Nambi."

Gulu said, "Kintu found food for himself when you took his cow away. Now we must test him again. He must prove that he is a good enough Man to marry the Daughter of the King of the Sky Country."

Gulu had his servants cook a meal that was enough food for a hundred people.

The Brother took the baskets of food to Kintu and said, "You can not marry my sister unless you can eat all of this food. If there is any food left in the morning, Gulu, the King of the Sky Country, will kill you."

Kintu ate as much food as he could. But he could not eat all of the food.

Kintu discovered a hole in the floor. He put the food that he could not eat into the hole and covered it up.

Then he called the servants to come and get the baskets that they used to bring the food.

Nambi's Brother came in the morning. When he saw the empty baskets he went to the Father and said, "Kintu has eaten the food."

Gulu said, "Kintu is a good Man. I will test him once more. Now if he can pick out his cow from among the cows of the Sky Country cows, he can marry my Daughter. I know Nambi loves him very much. And I want her to be happy."

Gulu told Kintu that he had to pick out his cow from the other cows in the Sky Country.

Kintu was sure he could not pick out his cow for all the cows in the Sky Country looked very much alike.

Kintu sat in the field and he was very sad.

A Bee came to Kintu and said, "I will help you. Be sure to pick the cow on whose horns I am sitting."

Gulu and his Son came into the field with a herd of cows.

Kintu watched the Bee. It did not go to any cow and sit on her horns.

"Can you pick your cow out of this herd?" asked Gulu.

"My cow is not in this herd," said Kintu.

Gulu said to his Son, "Go and get another herd of cows."

The Brother brought some more cows into the field. The Bee went at once and sat on the horns of one of the cows.

Kintu put his hand on the cow. "This is my cow," he said.

"Kintu is a good Man. Nobody will ever fool him," said Gulu. "I am very pleased with him. And now he can marry my Daughter who loves him very much."

Gulu told Kintu and Nambi that they must hurry and go back to Earth before Death went with them.

"Death has always wanted to go to the Earth Country. And he can only bring unhappiness," said Gulu.

Nambi and Kintu got ready to go to the Earth Country. Gulu gave them many gifts to take to their new home and he said,

"You must hurry and do not come back for anything because if you return for any reason, Death will go with you."

Nambi had a pet chicken that she was taking to Earth. As she and Kintu were going home, she suddenly stopped.

"I did not bring any food for my pet chicken. I will hurry back and get some food for my pet. I will be careful that no one sees me."

"Your Father told you not to return or Death would follow us down to Earth," said Kintu. "He will bring unhappiness to the people on Earth. He has always wanted to go to Earth, but he did not know the way."

"No one will see me," said Nambi. "I must get some food for my pet chicken. I am afraid it cannot eat the food on Earth.

Nambi ran back and got some food for her pet chicken.

But Death saw her. He followed Nambi and Kintu as they went down to Earth. He was very careful that no one saw him.

Kintu had a farm with many cows. And Nambi had many beautiful children.

But one day Death came to the door and asked for one of Kintu's daughters,

"I need a cook," said Death. "Send me one of your daughters."

"I cannot do that," said Kintu. "What would Gulu, King of the Sky, say if I sent one of his granddaughters to be your cook?"

Death was very angry and went away and said to himself, "I will kill the children of Nambi and Kintu."

One by one Kintu's children

died. Nambi and Kintu were sad.

"Go to my Father," said Nambi. "He will help us."

Kintu went to the Sky Country and told Gulu that his grandchildren were dead.

Gulu sadly shook his head.

"When you and Nambi left the Sky Country, I told you not to come back for anything. But you let Nambi come back for food for her pet chicken. Therefore Death saw her and followed you to Earth. And now your children are dead."

"You are the Great Sky King. Can't you do something to help us on Earth?" cried Kintu.

Gulu sent Nambi's Brother to Earth to try to catch Death and bring him back to the Sky Country. But Death went into the Earth and the Brother could not catch him.

And ever since that day, Death has lived on the Earth and brings unhappiness to the people.

The Drum

Nzambi, Mother Earth, made the World and all the people in it. And the people went out into the world and made many villages.

The people who lived in Nzambi's village liked to dance. But Nzambi had made no drum for her people. And they could not dance.

A little bird called Wagtail, who lived in a village nearby, was the first to make a drum. When he played his drum, the people danced.

Nzambi heard the drum and said, "I, Nzambi, the Mother Earth have no drum. The people of my village cannot dance. Go Antelope and tell little Wagtail that the Mother Earth wants his drum."

Antelope went to Wagtail.

"Wagtail," said Antelope, "Nzambi, the Mother Earth, wants your drum."

"No," said Wagtail. "I cannot give Nzambi my drum for I made the drum myself."

"Give your drum to me," said Antelope. "I want to learn to beat it."

And he took Wagtail's drum.

Antelope ran away with the drum.

Wagtail said to his people, "Antelope has stolen my drum."

The people ran after Antelope and killed him. The women carried the meat to the village and cooked it. Then the people had a feast and danced.

When Antelope did not come back with the drum, Nzambi was very sad and cried, "Nzambi, who made everything in the World, should have the drum."

And every time she heard the beating of the drum, she went into her house and cried.

After a while, Nzambi said to Ox, "Ox, you are very big. Wagtail and all of his friends will be afraid of you. Go to the village where Wagtail lives and get me the drum."

Ox went to Wagtail's village.

"Wagtail," said Ox, "Nzambi, the Mother Earth, wants your drum."

"No," said Wagtail, "I cannot give Nzambi my drum, for I made the drum myself."

"Give your drum to me," said Ox, "I want to learn to beat it."

Wagtail gave Ox his drum, and Ox ran away with the drum.

Wagtail called his people and said, "Ox has stolen my drum."

Then the people ran after Ox and killed him. The people carried the meat to the village and had a great feast.

When Ox did not come back with the drum, Nzambi went into her house and cried.

A very small Ant came into Nzambi's house and said,

"I will get the drum for you."

"I sent Antelope and I sent Ox," said Nzambi. "But they could not get the drum for me. You, Ant, are so small, how can you get the drum?"

"I am so small that no one will notice me," said Ant.

And so Ant went to Wagtail's village. He waited until all the people were asleep. Then Ant stole the drum. He took the drum to Nzambi. Her people beat the drum and danced all night.

When Wagtail opened his eyes in the morning, he heard the beating of his drum.

"Listen, the people in Nzambi's village are dancing. Someone has stolen my drum," said Wagtail.

He ran to the house where the drum was kept. But he could not find it.

Then Wagtail called all the birds together.

"We will have to take the matter before the Prince," said Wagtail. "He will have to say to whom the drum belongs."

A message was sent to Nzambi to bring the drum and come before the Prince. The Prince must say to whom the drum belonged.

The next day Nzambi and her people brought the drum before the Prince. Wagtail came and said to the Prince,

"Oh Prince, I made a drum. Let Nzambi tell why she has taken it from me."

"Oh, Prince," said Nzambi. "My people wanted to dance and they had no drum. I heard the beating of a drum in the village that I had given to Wagtail.

"I sent Antelope to ask Wagtail to give me the drum. He killed Antelope. I sent Ox to ask Wagtail to give me the drum. He killed Ox. My people were sad. Then little Ant went and brought me the drum. My people danced and were happy.

"Surely, Oh Prince, since I am the Mother Earth and made all the people in the World, I should have the drum."

The Prince thought for a long time. Then he said,

"It is true, Mother Earth, that you made all of us. When you made us you left us free to live our own life. But you did not give anyone a drum. Wagtail made the drum himself. The drum belongs to Wagtail."

Since that time many people have learned to make drums. A man in every village has learned to beat the drum. And the people love to dance.

The Daughter of the Sun
and the Moon

The Young Man wanted the Daughter of Lord Sun and Lady Moon for his wife. He had saved the bag of gold for a wedding present. Then he wrote a letter.

"I, a Young Man on Earth send this bag of gold for a wedding present. As soon as I can I will come for my wife."

But the Young Man could find no way of getting to the Sky Country.

Frog who lived in the well said, "I will take the wedding present and the letter to the Sky Country."

"How can you get to the Sky Country?" said the Young Man.

The Frog took the letter and the bag of gold. He went to the bottom of the well.

Pretty soon the servants of Lord Sun came to the well to fill their jugs with water. They put their jugs into the well, and Frog took the bag of gold and the letter and jumped into one of jugs.

Frog was taken to the Sky Country and to the house of Lord Sun and Lady Moon.

The water jugs were kept in a room on a table.

The servants put the water jugs on the table. Frog jumped out and put the letter and the bag of gold upon the table. Then he hid in a corner of the room.

Lord Sun and Lady Moon came to get some water. They found the letter and the bag of gold.

Lord Sun called, "Did any of you put this letter and this bag of gold upon the table?"

"No, no," said the servants.

"Who can it be?" said Lady Moon. "I will have the servants make a feast for he must be hungry."

The servants brought many baskets of food, and a feast was put upon the table.

When everyone had gone from the room, Frog came out of the corner and ate all the food he could. Then he went to find the Daughter of Lord Sun and Lady Moon. He found her asleep in her room.

Now Frog knew Great Magic.

He sat beside the beautiful Princess and made Great Earth Magic. The girl's eyes dropped out. Frog put them carefully in a cloth and went back to the room where the water jugs were kept. He hid in the corner.

In the morning the beautiful Princess did not get up.

Lady Moon went to her Daughter's room and said, "Why do you not get up?"

"I cannot open my eyes," said the Daughter of Lord Sun and Lady Moon.

Lady Moon went to Lord Sun and said, "Our Daughter is very sick. She cannot open her eyes."

Lord Sun sent for Ngombo who knew everything that happened on the Earth and in the Sky Country.

Ngombo came and sat beside the beautiful Daughter. He closed his eyes and made great magic.

With his eyes closed Ngombo said, "I see on Earth the Husband of the Daughter of Lord Sun and Lady Moon. He loves your Daughter and wants his wife to come to him.

"There has been a magic spell put on the Daughter of Lord Sun and Lady Moon. She will die if she is not sent to Earth to be with her Husband."

When Lord Sun and Lady Moon heard what Ngombo said, Lord Sun knew what he had to do to save his Daughter. He must send her to be the wife of the Young Man who lived upon the Earth.

Lord Sun called his Wise Men and said, "You must take my Daughter to her Husband who lives upon the Earth. She will die if she stays in the Sky Country."

Frog knew everything that was said for he had Great Magic.

The next morning Frog got into a water jug. When the servants came to go for water, Frog was taken back to Earth. The servants put their jugs down in the water, and Frog jumped out and hid in the bottom of the well. But Frog was very careful not to hurt the eyes of the Daughter of Lord Sun and Lady Moon.

Lord Sun called Spider and told him to make a very large web.

"My Daughter must go down the Spider web to the Earth. Ngombo says that she must go to her Husband or she will surely die.

"Spider, make your web large and strong, so that nothing will happen to the Daughter of Lord Sun and Lady Moon."

Spider worked day and night. He made a large web. He made a strong web. The web reached from the Sky Country down to the Earth.

The Wise Men were then ready to help the beautiful Princess go down to Earth.

The Young Man came to the well and said to the Frog,

"I am very sad for I love the Princess of the Sky Country, and I wish to marry her."

"Tomorrow your Wife will come from the Sky Country and I will bring her to your house," said Frog.

But the Young Man could not believe what the Frog said.

"You do not speak the truth." said the Young Man.

"Make ready," said Frog, "for I have Great Magic. I will bring the Daughter of Lord Sun and Lady Moon to your house tomorrow night."

The next evening the Wise Men brought the Princess of the Sky Country to Earth and left her at the well.

The Wise Men went back to the Sky Country. They took the Spider web with them so that the people on Earth could not climb up to Sky Country.

The beautiful Princess could not see. And she did not know what to do. She sat down beside the well and cried.

Frog came out of the well and said, "Do not be afraid. I will take you to the house of your Husband."

Then Frog gave the girl her eyes and they went to the Young Man's house.

"Your Wife is here," said Frog. "Now you know that I have told the truth."

This is the story of how the Young Man who lived upon the Earth married the Daughter of Lord Sun and Lady Moon who lived in the Sky Country.

The Story Without an End

Once an Old Father had a beautiful Daughter. She was so beautiful that all the men in the village wanted to marry her. The Old Father said,

"I will give my Daughter as Wife to the man who does three things,

"First, he is to stay in a room full of mosquitoes without clothes.

"Second, he is to eat red hot peppers without showing any pain.

"Third, he is to tell a story that does not end."

Some men could stand the mosquitoes. Some men could stand the mosquitoes and the red hot peppers. But no one was able to tell a story that did not end.

The storyteller would start telling his story as the sun was coming up. All day he told his story. But when the sun was going down, the story would end.

One day a Farmer came into the village to sell his corn. In the Marketplace he heard about the Old Father who would give his beautiful Daughter as Wife to the man who could do three things.

The Farmer thought to himself. "I think that I can do the three things that the Old Father asks of the man who marries his beautiful Daughter.

"First, I think that I can stay in a room full of mosquitoes without any clothes.

"Second, I think that I can eat red hot peppers without showing any pain.

"Third, I think that I can tell a story that will not end."

The Farmer laughed to himself.

"I will have to fool the Old Father. Then I will take home his beautiful Daughter as my Wife."

When the Farmer had sold his corn in the Marketplace, he went to the Old Father's house and asked for his beautiful Daughter.

"I have come to marry your Daughter," said the Farmer.

"Do you think that you can do the three things that I ask of every man?" said the Old Father.

The Old Father had his servants take the Farmer to a room filled with mosquitoes. The servants were all bundled up in clothes so that the mosquitoes could not bite them. But the Farmer took off his clothes and the mosquitoes began to bite him.

"As I was coming to the village, I saw a very strange horse," said the Farmer to the servants.

"Did you ever see a horse that was green all over his body?" asked the Farmer and he passed his hand all over his body. The mosquitoes flew away.

"No, no," said the servants. "Tell us about the Green Horse."

"He had a white spot on his forehead," said the Farmer, and he hit his forehead with his hand.

The mosquitoes flew away.

"The Green Horse had a black spot here and a yellow spot there," said the Farmer.

The Farmer hit the black spot on his leg and the yellow spot on his arm. He drove the mosquitoes away without the servants knowing, for they were only interested in the story of the Green Horse.

When the time was up, the servants took the Farmer to the Old Father and said,

"This man did not mind the mosquitoes for he stood without any clothes and told us a story about a Green Horse."

The Old Father said, "Bring the red hot peppers. Let him eat them."

"May I eat the red peppers in the court-yard?" asked the Farmer.

The servants brought a rug and placed it in the courtyard. And the Farmer sat upon the rug. When no one was looking, the Farmer threw some corn around him. The chickens came to eat the corn.

When the servants brought the red hot peppers, the Farmer said, "These chickens are bothering me."

And as he ate the red hot peppers he said, "Shoo, shoo, shoo," to the chickens.

In this way the Farmer ate the red hot peppers without showing any pain.

Now came the time for the Farmer to tell a story that did not end.

The next morning when the sun was coming up, the Farmer began to tell how he planted his farm with corn. With his wooden hoe he dug a hole. He put one, two, three grains of corn into the hole.

And then he dug another hole and planted one, two, three grains of corn in that hole. And so on and so on.

The sun was overhead before all the corn was planted.

Then the Farmer told how three little green leaves came up in one hole. And then how three little green leaves came up in another hole.

The sun was going down before all the little green leaves on the farm had come up.

The Old Father was getting very sleepy. But the Farmer kept on telling how the corn stocks grew taller and taller. And how the ears of corn came upon the corn stocks and turned yellow. The corn was ripe. All night Farmer told how he picked the corn and took it to the barn.

The Old Father was very sleepy and could hardly keep his eyes open. He thought that now the corn was in the barn, surely the Farmer's story would end.

But when the sun came up for the second day, the Farmer said,

"I saw a little mouse running around the barn.

"The little mouse picked up a grain of corn in his mouth and ran to a small hole. Pretty soon he came out of the hole and picked up another grain of corn in his mouth and ran back to the small hole."

The Old Father went to sleep. When he woke up the Farmer was still saying,

"The mouse picked up another grain of corn in his mouth and ran back to the small hole."

"Stop," cried the Old Father.

"But you have not heard the end of my story," said the Farmer.

"I will never live long enough to hear the end of your story. You have won my beautiful Daughter for your Wife," said the Old Father.

The Farmer took his beautiful Wife home with him. And he was very happy.

The Lost Daughter

There was a King who lived a long time ago. He had many children. But he did not want any more daughters.

The King's Wife was going to have a child. King said, "If a girl child should be born, it must be thrown into the river and drowned."

Then the King went on a long hunting trip for he did not want to hear the crying of his Queen if a baby girl was born.

When the child was born, it was a beautiful little girl.

"Your Father does not want you," the Queen said to the baby.

The Queen took the child to the river. But she could not throw it into the water. She carried the baby into the forest.

As the Queen walked in the forest, she saw a parrot.

"Beautiful Parrot," said the Queen. "How can I save my baby girl? The King wants me to throw her into the river and drown her."

"I do not know how to help you," said the parrot. "Ask the next parrot that you see."

Pretty soon the Queen saw another parrot. He was more beautiful than the first parrot.

"Beautiful Parrot, tell me how can I save my baby girl."

"I do not know how to help you," said the parrot. "Ask the next parrot that you see. He is greater than I am."

As the Queen walked in the forest, the biggest and most beautiful parrot in the world flew to her.

"Please tell me, Beautiful Parrot," cried the Queen, "how can I save my baby girl? The King wants me to drown her in the river."

"Give your baby to me," said the parrot. "I will take her to the Old Grandmother. But bring a banana stalk and two pieces of sugar cane."

The Queen gave the baby to the parrot. She put the banana stalk and the sugar cane by the baby.

The parrot flew to the Old Grandmother's house and laid the baby and the banana stalk and the two pieces of sugar cane in the Old Grandmother's lap.

"This is a present from the Wife of the King," said the parrot. "Tell no one that she is a Princess."

Year by year the little girl

grew to be a beautiful woman. The bananas and sugar cane grew in the garden and gave the Grandmother and the Princess their food.

The Grandmother was getting very old. She knew that she must send the Princess back to her Mother.

The Grandmother had the servants make a big canoe. She made mats from the leaves of the sugar cane for the Princess to sit upon. She put bananas in the canoe for food. And she made the Princess a drum.

The Grandmother said, "You are

going to your Father, the King
and your Mother, the Queen."

The Princess got in the canoe
and beat her drum. She sang,

"I go away, I go away
But my love is here
With my Grandmother."

As the Princess went down the
river, she sang,

"Listen, all you people
To the song I sing
I am the King's
    daughter
Who lived with her
    Grandmother."

The Princess beat her drum and sang

"And home I return
When my little drum
Tells the King
I have come."

Some fishermen heard the song. They came near in their canoe and saw the beautiful Princess. "I will go and tell the King that his daughter is coming," said one of the fishermen.

The fisherman told the King that his daughter was coming down the river in a big canoe. But the King did not believe him.

The King sent a Wise Man to look at the girl. The Wise Man came back and said, "This girl is the most beautiful in the world."

Then the King got into his big canoe and went up the river. Soon he heard the Princess singing,

> "Listen, all you people
>   I am the King's
>   daughter
>   Who lived with her
>   Grandmother
>   And home I return
>   When my little drum
>   Tells the King
>   I have come."

When the King came near the Princess, he called, "Who are you?"

"I am the daughter of the King of this country," said the Princess. "I am going to the King, my Father, and my Mother."

When the King saw how beautiful the Princess was, he said, "I am the King of the country. I will take you home."

The canoes were quickly paddled to the shore of the King's village. But the Princess would not get out of her canoe.

"Put down a mat of grass. It is not right for a Princess to step upon the ground."

The servants put down a mat of grass. And the Princess walked along the mat of grass all the way to her Mother's house.

The Queen said to the King, "I did not drown the beautiful baby girl. I gave it to the parrot in the forest.

"The parrot took my child to my Grandmother with a banana stalk and two pieces of sugar cane so that they would have food.

"Grandmother took care of the baby. She grew to be a beautiful Princess. And now she has come home to her Father and her Mother."

The King was very happy that his beautiful daughter had not been drowned in the river.

He had his servants make a great feast. The people beat the drums and danced and sang. The people were very happy.

But the King and the Queen were the happiest because they had the Princess back.

Little Kibatti

Kibatti was a little boy. He lived with his Mother and his Father just outside the village.

One night he heard a strange noise. He got up and went to the door of the hut. He heard the cries of the people in the village.

The big animals were pushing over the huts in the village. They were killing the people.

Kibatti ran to his Mother and his Father.

"Wake up! Wake up!" cried Kibatti. "The big animals are killing all the people in the village. We must leave our hut and run to the forest. We must climb the highest tree that we can find."

Kibatti and his Mother and his Father ran to the forest.

Soon they were all up in the highest tree in the forest. They were very much afraid. They could hear the cries of the people in the village.

Kibatti said, "We will have to stay up in the tree all night. But we are safe for the animals cannot see us."

In the morning, Kibatti saw that there was not a hut left in the village. All the people were dead. Only big animals were walking in the streets.

"I am going down to see if there is anything that I can do," said Kibatti. "I am so small that no one will notice me if I am quiet."

"Be very careful," said his Mother.

Kibatti went to the village. He watched the animals. They were cleaning up the village.

Kibatti picked out the Chief Elephant and the Chief Buffalo and the Chief Rhinoceros and the Chief Lion and the Chief Leopard.

"If I could kill the Chiefs the other animals would run back to the forest," said Kibatti to himself. Kibatti went to the high tree in the forest. He told his Mother and his Father what he had seen.

"The animals have killed all the people in the village. They have pushed over the huts."

"What are we to do," asked the Mother.

"We must stay up in this tree for here we are safe," said Kibatti.

"We cannot stay up in this tree forever," said the Father. "We would die."

"I have a plan to kill the Chiefs," said Kibatti. "If their Chiefs are dead, the other animals will run back to the forest."

"Tell me your plan and I will help you," said his Father.

"Tonight the Chiefs will stand in the village," said Kibatti. "We will pay a visit to the Chiefs."

In the middle of the night, Kibatti and his Father climbed down from the tree. They went to their hut outside the village.

Kibatti found ropes and two rope nets, and his hunting knife, and five of his Father's spears. He also carefully carried an egg.

"Father, take your spears and stay in the forest," said Kibatti. "But come quickly when I call."

Kibatti went to the village and left the rope nets outside.

The Chief Buffalo was guarding the gate.

"Hello, Hello," called Kibatti. "Can you let a little boy come in for the night is very cold."

Buffalo was very sleepy.

"Who are you?" asked Buffalo.

"A Forest Child," said Kibatti.

"What do you want?" asked Buffalo.

"Only a little fire to cook my egg and a place to sleep."

"Wait here," said Buffalo. "I must talk to the other animals."

Buffalo went to the other Chiefs and woke them up.

"What shall we do about the boy," asked Buffalo.

"Is he a boy of the village who was not killed?" asked Rhinoceros.

"No," said Elephant. "If he had been a boy of the village, he would have known what had happened to the people of the village."

Lion and Leopard both said, "A little boy will do no harm. Tomorrow we can kill him. But now let us go to sleep."

Buffalo went back to the gate.

"Come in Forest Child. You can stay for the night."

"Thank you," said Kibatti, "In the morning I will go back to the forest."

The Buffalo lay down and went to sleep.

Kibatti came through the gate but he did not go to sleep. He took his rope and tied Buffalo's feet together.

Kibatti found Elephant sleeping against a tree. He tied Elephant's feet together. But Elephant did not wake up. He found Rhinocerous and tied his feet together.

Kibatti went very quickly out of the gate and got his two rope nets. He put one rope net over Lion and tied it to the fence.

He found Leopard sleeping by the fence. He put a net over Leopard and tied it to the fence.

The animals did not wake up.

Kibatti ran to the forest and called, "Father, come quickly and bring your spears. We are going to kill the Chiefs. Then the other animals will leave the village and go back to the forest."

Father killed Buffalo with his spear. He killed Elephant and he killed Rhinocerous.

By now the Lion was awake and roaring. Father killed the Lion with his spear.

Father took his last spear and killed the Leopard.

In the morning, the animals saw that their Chiefs were dead. They left the village and went back to the forest.

Kibatti and his Father went back to the tree in the forest.

Kibatti called, "Mother, you can come down from the tree. You are safe now."

Then Kibatti and his Father and his Mother went down the road to the next village.

The people of the next village
gave them food. They sat around
the fire. Father told the story
of how the Chiefs of the animals
were killed. The people of the
village cried, "Little Kibatti is
the bravest man we know."

The Man Who Did Not Freeze

There was a rich man whose name was Haptom. He had lands and cattle. He had fine houses and beautiful wives. He had every thing that money could buy. But he could find nothing that interested him.

Haptom had a servant whose name was Arha. He was very poor. But he did his work well and he was a happy man.

One cold night Haptom told Arha to build a fire.

"I wonder how cold it must get before a man freezes," said Haptom.

Arha said, "I do not know," and went on building the fire.

"If a man stood on top of a mountain all night long without any fire and without any clothes would he freeze to death?" asked Haptom.

"I do not know," said Arha. "But I think that he would be very foolish."

"I bet a man could not do it," said Haptom.

"I have nothing to bet," said Arha. "But I think a strong man could do it."

And now for the first time in a year the rich man was much interested in something.

"I will make a bet with you Arha. If you can stand all night on top of a mountain without any fire and without any clothes to keep you warm, I will give you a farm and a house and cattle."

Arha could hardly believe what Haptom said.

"I would do anything for my own farm," said Arha.

"It is a bet," said Haptom.

Then he called two servants and told them to take Arha to the top of the mountain the next night.

Haptom said to the servants, "See that Arha stands on top of the mountain all night without fire and without clothes to keep him warm."

The next day Arha went to see an Old Man who was his friend.

"I think that I have made a very foolish bet," said Arha. "I told Haptom that I could stand on top of a mountain all night without fire and without clothes."

The Old Man said, "I will help you. Tonight I will build a fire on top of a big rock in the valley that you can see from the mountain. Never take your eyes off the fire."

"Remember what I tell you," said the Old Man. "Think of nothing but how warm that fire feels. Never shut your eyes and never stop thinking how warm the fire feels. You will not freeze to death."

That night the servants took Arha to the top of the mountain. He took off his clothes and stood in the cold wind. He looked down in the valley and saw the fire that the Old Man had built on the big rock.

Ahra never took his eyes from the fire in the valley. He thought how wise the Old Man was. He thought how warm the fire felt.

The next morning the servants took Ahra to Haptom.

"He stood on the mountain all night without fire and without clothes," said the servants.

"You are a very strong man," said Haptom. "How did you do it?"

"All night I watched a fire in the valley," said Arha. "I thought how warm the fire felt."

"You were to be without fire," cried Haptom. "You lose the bet."

"But the fire was down in the valley and could not warm me," said Arha.

"It was only the fire that saved you," said Haptom.

Arha went to his friend and said, "Haptom says that the fire in the valley kept me warm and that I did not win the bet."

"Tell the Judge your story," said the Old Man. "Let him say if you have lost the bet."

Arha told his story to the Judge.

The Judge sent for Haptom and his two servants.

Haptom told the Judge about his bet with Arha. The servants told the Judge that Arha had watched a fire in the valley all night.

The Judge said, "Arha, you have lost the bet, for Haptom said that you must do without fire."

Arha went to his friend, the Old Man and said, "I will have to be a servant all of my life. I will never have a farm of my own."

The Old Man said, "I think I can help you. For the fire in the valley could not have warmed you."

When the Old Man had been young he had been a servant to a rich man named Hailu. He went to Hailu and told him about Arha.

"The Judge was wrong," said Hailu. "The fire in the valley could not have warmed Arha on the top of the mountain. I think that I can help your friend, for he is poor and Haptom is rich."

Hailu who was a very important man invited many guests to come to his house for a feast.

Haptom and the Judge were among the guests invited to the feast.

When the day of the feast came, they dressed in their best clothes for Hailu was a very rich man. There was always the best of food at his feast.

The guests sat around on beautiful rugs for Hailu's house was the finest in the village.

From the kitchen came the smell of good food. And the guests grew very hungry.

Music was played and beautiful girls danced. But the servants did not serve the guests any food.

The guests looked at each other. They did not know what to say for never before had they been invited to a feast without food.

At last Haptom, who was very hungry said, "Hailu, why have you asked us to a feast and yet your servants do not serve us any food?"

Hailu smiled and said, "My dear friend Haptom, if Arha was warmed by the fire he watched in the valley, then you have been fed by the good smells from my kitchen."

The Judge said, "I see I was wrong when I said that Arha lost the bet with Haptom."

Haptom said, "Hauli you are a very wise man. Arha has won the bet and I give him a farm and a house and some cattle."

Then the servants brought the food and there was a wonderful feast.

The Two Brothers

There were once two brothers who quarreled all of the time.

"I am wiser than you," said the Younger Brother.

"You are a fool," said the Older Brother.

At last the Younger Brother was so angry that he took his wife and left the village. They wandered in the forest.

They came to a stream of clear water. And they sat down to rest.

After the Younger Brother and his Wife had rested, they went up the stream and found a small village.

"Let us go back to our village," said the Wife. "These people may hurt us."

"No," said the Younger Brother. "I will not go back to our village. My Older Brother called me a fool."

The Younger Brother and his Wife went into the village. They found only three huts for there was one man and his wives and his children who lived in the village.

"Where do you come from," said the Man.

"I come from a village in the forest," said the Younger Brother.

"Are you a bad man for I do not want a bad man in my village."
"No," said the Younger Brother. "But I quarreled with my Older Brother. I do not want to live in my village any longer."

"You may live here," said the Man. "For I too have quarreled with my people.

"You and your Wife may have one of the huts and stay with me."

The Younger Brother and his Wife made their Home in the village.

One day the Man came to the Younger Brother and said,

"We must go into the forest and kill an animal for food. Come with me and help me dig a pit. We will cover the pit with brush. Soon an animal will fall into the deep pit, and we will have meat to eat."

The two men went into the forest. They worked hard all day. They made the pit very deep and covered it with brush. At night they went back to the village.

"When we catch some animals, how are we going to divide them?" said the Man.

The Young Man said, "There are female animals and there are male animals. I will take the male animals. You can take the female animals that fall into the pit."

"We do not want to quarrel," said the Man. "I will take the female animals and you shall have the male animals."

The next morning the two men went to see if any animal had fallen into the pit. They found a male animal.

"The male animal is yours," said the Man to the Younger Brother. And the Younger Brother took the animal home to his Wife.

Each morning the two men went to the pit. Each morning they found a male animal in the pit. And each day the Younger Brother took the animal home to his wife.

The Younger Brother's hut was filled with more meat than he and his Wife could eat.

The Man wanted some meat for his wives and children. But the Younger Brother did not give any of the meat to the Man.

The Younger Brother said to his Wife, "Go into the forest and get some wood to make a fire. We must smoke this meat so that we can keep it."

The Wife went into the forest. She did not come back at night.

The Younger Brother went to the Man and said, "My Wife has not come back home from the forest."

"It is dark now and we cannot see," said the Man. "In the morning I will go with you into the forest and hunt for your Wife."

The Younger Brother could not sleep that night because he kept thinking about his Wife. He was afraid some animal might have killed her.

In the morning the Man came to the Younger Brother's hut and said,

"I will help you find your Wife."

When the two men came to the deep pit in the forest, they found the Wife in the bottom of the pit.

"I have been in the pit all night," cried the Wife. "Come and get me out of this deep pit."

The Younger Brother was going to jump down into the pit.

"No", cried the Man. "Your Wife is a female and she belongs to me. I can do what I like with her."

The two men quarreled all day. But the Man always said, "Your Wife is a female. She belongs to me and I can do what I like with her."

Now it happened that the Older Brother had gone hunting in the forest. He got lost. Then he heard his Brother's voice. And he went to find his Brother.

When the Younger Brother saw his Older Brother he said, "I am glad to see you. I want to tell you how sorry I am that I quarreled with you."

Then the Younger Brother told his story to his Older Brother.

"My Wife is in the bottom of the pit. The Man says that because she is female, he can do with her what he likes. The Man may kill my Wife."

"The Man is right," said the Older Brother. "You agreed that he could have the female animals. And your Wife is a female. He had better jump into the pit and kill her."

"You are very wise," said the Man as he jumped into the pit.

The Younger Brother cried out and was going to jump into the pit after the Man. But the Older Brother held him back.

"Don't be a fool," said the Older Brother. "The Man is in the pit and he is a male. Therefore he is yours. You can do anything you want with him.

"If you do not kill the Man, I think that he will give your Wife back to you," said the Older Brother.

"Older Brother, you are wiser than I am," said the Younger Brother.

The two brothers helped the Man and the Wife out of the deep pit.

And then the two brothers and the Wife went back to their village.

The Prince Who Wanted the Moon

Once there was a King who was very sad. All his children were girls. The King wanted a son very much.

Then one day a son was born to the King's youngest Wife. And the King was very happy.

The baby grew up to be a fine strong boy. The King loved the little boy so much that he gave him everything he wanted. But the little boy was not happy.

One day the Prince was playing with his friends.

"There is nothing that my Father, the King, would not give to me. He will give me anything that I want."

A little boy said to the Prince, "I know something that your Father cannot give to you."

This made the Prince very angry and he said in a loud voice,

"My Father, the King, can give me anything that I want for he is a most powerful King."

The little boy laughed. He said, "Your Father cannot give you the Moon."

Then all the children laughed. The Prince was very angry. He started to cry. He went to his Father, the King, and said,

"Father you have given me everything that I wanted. But I will never be happy until you give me the Moon."

The King was very much surprised and said,

"My Son, the Moon is very far away. Nobody can get the Moon."

The Prince began to cry and he said, "Father you are the most powerful King. You can get anything for me. If you don't get me the Moon, I shall die."

The King did not know what to do. He could not get the Prince to stop crying. The Prince would not eat anything. He would not go out and play with the other children.

The King called all his Wise Men together. He asked them if anyone could tell him how to get the Moon for the little Prince.

"I will give half of my Kingdom to anyone who can get the Moon for me," said the King.

"The Moon is high in the Sky. I have never been higher in the Sky than the highest tree," said one Wise Man.

"I have never been higher in the Sky than the highest Mountain," said another Wise Man. "And the Moon is far above the highest Mountain."

One by one the Wise Men went home. Only the youngest Wise Man was left.

At last he said, "Oh King, I only live to do what you wish. I will try and get the Moon for you. But I will need the help of all the people in your Kingdom."

"Ask me for anything and it shall be yours," said the King. "Only get me the Moon so that the Prince will not die."

The King called all his people together. "Hear all my people what the young Wise Man tells you. He is going to get me the Moon for the Prince so he will not die. The young Wise Man wishes you to help him. Everyone is to do just what he tells them to do."

"We will build a scaffold on the highest Mountain," said the young Wise Man. "We will build another scaffold on top of it. Some day we will reach the Moon.

"The men will cut down the trees in the forest and carry them to the top of the highest Mountain. There we will make the scaffold."

Then the young Wise Man said to the women, "You will cook and make bread for the men. The boys will carry food and water to the men in the forest and to the men on top of the Mountain. The girls will plant the gardens."

Every one in the Kingdom worked for the young Wise Man and helped him build a scaffold on the top of the highest Mountain.

Day by day the people built the scaffold. At the end of the year, the scaffold was so high in the Sky you could not see the top.

The people all thought that they could reach the Moon.

People from other Kingdoms came to see the wonderful thing that the King and his people had built. They thought the King was mad. They whispered among themselves,

"This is a bad thing that the King is doing. If anything happens to the Moon, the people on Earth will be killed. Let us go far away."

Then the young Wise Man came to the King and said, "Oh King, I have come to tell you that now we can reach the Moon."

The King was very pleased. "I will go with you to the top of the scaffold and help to bring the Moon down to Earth."

"I must go too," cried the Prince. "It is my Moon and I want to bring it down to Earth."

And so the King and the Prince and the young Wise Man started to the top of the scaffold.

Day after day they climbed. Week after week they climbed. It took them a year to get to the top of the scaffold.

The King reached out his hand and touched the Moon.

"Oh, Oh," cried the King. "The Moon is very hot. My Son, you cannot play with anything so hot."

"I want it, I want it," cried the Prince. "It is my Moon."

The young Wise Man put a rope of green vines around the Moon. He pulled so hard, he cracked the Moon.

All the fire in the Moon poured out. It burnt up the King and the Prince and the young Wise Man. It burnt up the scaffold. The fire rolled over the Earth like a river. It burnt up everything on the Earth.

Some of the men and women were saved because they were turned into gorillas. And some of the children were saved because they were turned into monkeys. They ran away to another Kingdom.

Now some night when the Moon is round, you can see the cracks where the fire came out of the Moon.

And if you watch the gorillas and the monkeys, you will see that they do not give their children everything that the children want. A wise father gives a child only that which is good for him.

The Two Wives

Once upon a time, a long time ago, a man had two wives. One wife was beautiful and good. One wife was lazy and selfish. Each wife had a daughter. And each daughter was just like her mother.

The good wife went into the village to sell palm oil. And her daughter whose name was Alake went with her.

Alake and her Mother walked and walked. At last they sold some palm oil to a man.

"I find that I have no money to pay for this palm oil. Come to my house and I will get some money to pay you. But my house is far away," the Man said.

Alake and her Mother had worked hard to get the palm oil and earn some money. The Mother said,

"We will come with you even if your house is far away."

But Alake and her Mother did not know that the Man was a Spirit who had come down to Earth.

At last they came to the Man's house. The Man went into his house and got some money to pay for the palm oil. The Man told Alake to go into his garden and pick three gourds.

"Some are pretty yellow gourds, said the Man. "And some are not pretty.

"Pick three of the gourds that are not pretty and take them home with you.

"When you get near your village, break the first gourd. When you get to your garden, break the second gourd. When you get inside your hut, break the third gourd."

"Thank you," said Alake. She went to the garden and picked three large gourds that were not pretty.

Alake and her Mother walked to their village. They were very tired for the gourds were heavy and it was a long walk.

Alake did just as the Man had told her to do. When she was near the village, she broke the first gourd. Many servants came out of the gourd to help them on their way home.

When Alake came to her garden, she broke the second gourd. Boxes of fine dresses and beautiful beads came out of the gourd. The servants carried the boxes of fine dresses and beautiful beads into Alake's hut.

The whole village was surprised to see Alake and her Mother coming home with such riches.

When Alake was inside her hut, she broke the third gourd. Gold poured out of the gourd.

Alake divided all the riches into three parts.

Alake gave one part of her riches to her Father. She gave another part to the lazy wife and her daughter. And she and her Mother kept the third part. They were all rich.

But the lazy wife and the selfish daughter, whose name was Abeo, wanted more riches.

"Let us go to the village and sell palm oil," said Abeo. "Maybe we will meet the Man that gave Alake presents."

The next day Abeo and her Mother went to the village to sell palm oil. They met the Man who was a Spirit.

The Man said to Abeo and her Mother, "I want to buy your palm oil but I have no money with me. Will you come to my house so that I can get some money. It is a long walk."

They wanted to go with the Man because they thought that he would give them some presents.

They walked and walked. At last they came to the Man's house. The Man went into the house and got some money to pay for the palm oil.

The Man told Abeo to go into his garden and pick three gourds. "Some are pretty yellow gourds. And some are not pretty," said the Man. "Pick three gourds that are not pretty, and take them home with you. When you get near your village, break the first gourd. When you get to your garden, break the second gourd. And when you get inside your hut, break the third gourd."

Abeo's Mother was very happy. "We will have wonderful presents," she said to herself.

Abeo did not even say "Thank you." She ran to the garden and picked three of the prettiest yellow gourds that she could find.

"I am sure the pretty gourds will have better presents in them," Abeo said to her Mother.

Abeo and her Mother started for their village. They walked and walked. They were very tired for the gourds were heavy and it was a long walk to their village.

The Mother said, "I am very tired. I am going to sit down and rest."

"These gourds are very heavy," said Abeo. "Why should we carry them all the way to the village? I am going to break one now."

Abeo and her Mother broke the first gourd. Bees came out of the gourd and started to sting them.

Abeo and her Mother picked up the other gourds and started to run. They ran as fast as they could to the village.

The whole village was surprised to see Abeo and her Mother running through the village with bees flying after them. "Kill the bees," cried Abeo. They are hurting us."

When Abeo and her Mother got to their garden, they broke the second gourd. A big monkey came out of the gourd and beat them with a stick.

Abeo and her Mother ran into their hut and shut the door.

"Surely the third gourd will have gold in it," said the Mother.

Abeo broke the third gourd. A big snake came out of the gourd. The snake bit Abeo and the snake bit the Mother. They lay down and died.

That was the end of two lazy selfish people.